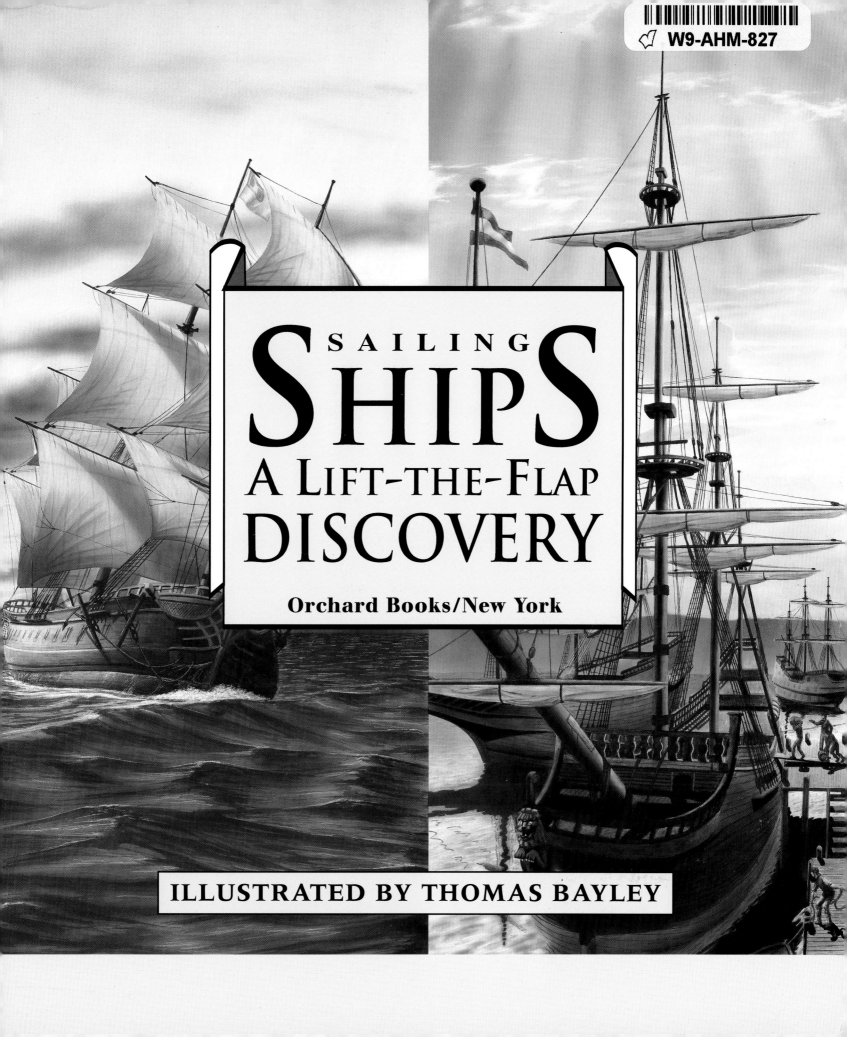

Sailing SHIPS
A Lift-the-Flap DISCOVERY

Orchard Books/New York

ILLUSTRATED BY THOMAS BAYLEY

Santa María

The *Santa María* was the largest of three ships in the 1492 expedition of Christopher Columbus, in which he discovered America. It was a small carrack, or galleon, commanded by Columbus himself. His other two ships, the *Niña* and the *Pinta*, were smaller caravels.

Columbus

Columbus was an adventurer from Genoa, Italy. He convinced the rulers of Castile, in Spain, to let him look for a direct route to Asia by sailing west. It took him eight years to get their approval!

A new route was very attractive. The Moors, who were Muslim, controlled all of the eastern trade routes, and their relations with the European Christian states were worsening.

The Voyage

The ships sailed on August 3, 1492, but stopped in the Canary Islands, off the coast of Africa, to repair a rudder. From there they sailed again on September 6. They crossed unknown seas for thirty-one days, out of sight of land. Ships usually kept close to the coastline on voyages. The crews wanted to turn back, as most men believed the world was flat and that the ships would reach the edge and fall off. On October 12, lookouts spotted land. This was the island now known as Watling Island in the Bahamas. Columbus believed he had reached Asia. He named the new land San Salvador.

Astrolabe

The Indies

Columbus sailed around Cuba and Jamaica. On Christmas Day, the *Santa María* hit a reef off La Española (now Haiti and the Dominican Republic) and sank. Columbus sailed for Spain, leaving forty-three men behind. He could not fit them on the two remaining ships. Convinced they were in the Indian Ocean, they called the islands the Indies.

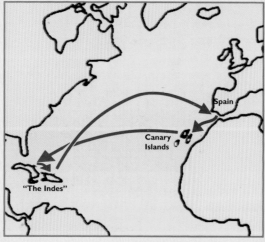
The route of the *Santa María*

Disgrace

Columbus made three more voyages to the Indies in 1493, 1498, and 1503. All were failures. He commanded a fleet of seventeen ships on the first, but found that the men left behind the previous year were dead, killed by the local inhabitants. In 1498, he reached Venezuela. This success was overshadowed by dissatisfaction with his settlements in La Española. He was disgraced and returned to Spain in chains. Columbus made one last voyage, in 1502, to Central America. He died in 1506, almost forgotten.

Sails

Carracks had three masts. One large square sail, with a smaller topsail, was set on the middle mainmast and a smaller square sail on the foremast at the bow, or front, of the ship. The crew hoisted a lateen sail, a triangular-shaped one hung from a cross spar, or wooden pole, on the stern-, or mizzenmast, at the rear of the ship. Smaller caravels were lateen rigged on all three masts, although some ships had a square sail on the foremast.

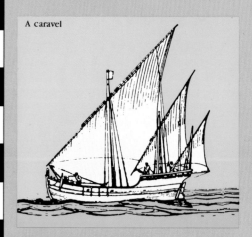
A caravel

Navigation

To measure the ship's speed, the navigator dropped a piece of wood at the bow, or front of the ship, and recorded the time it took to reach the stern, the back of the ship. The compass, a spinning magnetized needle that turned to the magnetic north pole, was first used by seamen in the twelfth century. This gave the direction of the ship. With direction and speed known, the pilot plotted the position of the ship by putting a peg into a traverse board every half hour. He also recorded the changing position of the stars with an astrolabe to help pinpoint the ship's position.

Mayflower

The *Mayflower* was the ship in which the Pilgrims sailed to America in 1620. With Captain Christopher Jones in command, it set out from England on September 16. The Pilgrims planned to settle in the colony of Virginia, but bad weather and poor navigation drove them north.

Two months into the voyage, on November 19, the Pilgrims sighted land at Cape Cod, Massachusetts. They landed at the site of Plymouth on December 26. The Pilgrims were several hundred miles away from their planned destination. Altogether, the voyage had taken 103 days.

The Ship

The *Mayflower* was a small ship. Her frame consisted of strong oak beams, over which were laid oak planks. She had two main decks above the hold, or cargo area, with a raised deck, called the *poop*, in the stern. This was above the captain's cabin.

Sails

Information about the design of the *Mayflower* is sketchy, but there were probably three masts. The builders of the ship hung square sails from spars that were set at right angles to the masts. These sails drove the ship. The crew could also raise a lateen sail at the stern of the ship. Moving these sails with ropes helped to steer the *Mayflower* through the water.

Steering

One person, called the helmsman, was responsible for steering the ship. He could change the angle of the sails to the mast, by pulling in or letting out rope joined to the spars, and he could move the ship's rudder. To do this he pushed a very large lever, called a *whipstaff*, from side to side. The whipstaff was linked to the rudder, which was positioned in the water at the stern. The water flowing past the rudder changed the direction of the ship.

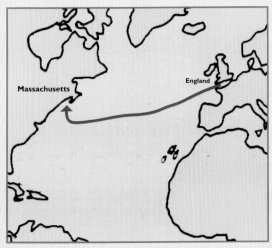

The route of the *Mayflower*

Passengers

The Pilgrims were part of a sixteenth-century Puritan sect. They believed in a simple life, simple worship, and strict religious discipline. They were outcasts from the English Protestant movement, which did not like these simple beliefs. So they set out to make a new life in America.

The Pilgrims arrived at Plymouth in the middle of winter. Weak, half-starved, and unhealthy from the voyage, they lacked food in their new home. The hard winter that followed their arrival killed half of them very quickly.

Life on Board

The *Mayflower* was a merchant ship before it was converted to carry the Pilgrims. She had transported cargoes of cloth and wine. Conditions were very cramped and uncomfortable for the passengers. The Pilgrims included forty-four men, nineteen women, twenty-nine boys, and ten girls. In addition, there were forty-seven crew members crowded on board.

Cargo

The ship was packed with all the things the Pilgrims needed to form a settlement on their arrival. The cargo included furniture, building and gardening tools, and seeds. There was a printing press as well as some goats and chickens. The ship carried supplies for the long voyage, including barrels of water, salted beef, vegetables, bread, and beer.

Health

The voyage took much longer than planned because of frequent storms, high seas, and poor navigation. The Pilgrims were half-starved, and the *Mayflower* was an unhealthy place in which to live. Space was so short that everyone on board had to sleep wherever they could. The top decks leaked, and the Pilgrims were constantly wet from seawater. The bad weather also meant that the Pilgrims had to use buckets as toilets below decks. These terrible conditions caused disease and sickness.

Santa María

Length
80 feet *(Santa María)*
50 feet *(Pinta* and *Niña)*

Width
26 feet *(Santa María)*
16 feet *(Pinta* and *Niña)*

Weight
102 tons *(Santa María)*
59 tons *(Pinta* and *Niña)*

Mainmast
77 feet *(Santa María)*
48 feet *(Pinta* and *Niña)*

Sails
Square-rigged mainmast and foremast.
Lateen-sail sternmast *(Santa María)*.
Lateen sails *(Pinta* and *Niña)*. The *Niña*
was rerigged with square sails for the
return journey.

Crew
90 men *(Santa María)*
18 men (on both *Pinta* and
Niña)

Weapons
Muskets for the crew

BATAVIA

The *Batavia* was one of many heavily armed merchant ships. These "East Indiamen" carried cargo from India and East Asia to Europe.

A Dutch ship built to carry cargo, passengers, sailors, soldiers, and all the supplies they needed on a long voyage of many months, the *Batavia* was also well armed to resist attack from other warships and pirates.

EAST INDIA COMPANIES

At the beginning of the seventeenth century, trade with India and East Asia was controlled by the Portuguese. Their sea explorers had discovered these rich markets. The trade routes to the East were chains of ports and islands they had colonized. Still, by 1606, all the great European sea powers were trying to grab the largest part of this trade for themselves.

They formed powerful trading companies: the English in 1600, the Dutch in 1602, the Danish in 1616, and the French in 1664. Each company was a military and a trading power. These companies and their ships dominated trade with the East for 250 years. Ships were well armed and included soldiers and sailing crews on board.

TRADE AND WAR

The Dutch United East India Company set out to capture the ports held by the Portuguese, and by 1656 it had succeeded and controlled the spice trade. The English were just as interested in exporting their woolen goods as they were in importing cargo from the East. But by 1650 Dutch ships landed most cargoes in England. The Navigation Act of 1651 prohibited ships from foreign ports from loading or unloading in England. War broke out between the two sea powers. Sea battles took place between 1652 and 1673, and the French also became involved. The French fleet defeated the Dutch in 1676 – a defeat that left England as the major sea power.

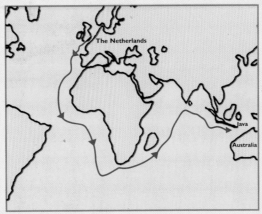

The route of the *Batavia*

RIGGING

Rigging, the ropes and blocks used to support the masts and control the sails, were of two types. Standing rigging secured the masts at front and back with ropes called *stays*. Side ropes, called *shrouds*, prevented sideways movement. Running rigging, ropes that ran through blocks, controlled the sails. The mainstay, the most important support, was six inches thick.

Because the Dutch had a huge navy and a small population, they were short of seamen. One out of every five Dutchmen was a sailor or fisherman. As a result, they simplified the rigging of their ships, setting just two sails on each mast to make them easier to handle.

BUILDING THE SHIP

Oak was used to build the main frame of the ship. The master shipbuilder chose different woods for other parts. He made the mast, decks, and the sterncastle from pine because it was much lighter than oak. The *Batavia* carried important passengers to and from the East, and luxury cabins were included in the ship.

DISASTER

The *Batavia* was built in 1628. On her maiden, or first, voyage in 1629, she sank between Java, now Indonesia, and Australia. Most of the crew and passengers reached land. Because the waters around their coast were very shallow, Dutch ships had very shallow drafts. Only sixteen feet of the hull was below the water line. Big ships like the *Batavia* were, therefore, less stable in high winds.

Mayflower

Length
96.5 feet

Width
26 feet

Weight
198 tons

Mainmast
97 feet

Sails
Square rigged

Crew
47 men

Weapons
A few cannon for defense

BOUDEUSE

The *Boudeuse* was the ship in which the great French seaman Comte Louis Antoine de Bougainville circled the world from December 1766 to March 1769. He was the first Frenchman to do so. Only seven out of two hundred men who sailed on the *Boudeuse* and its store ship, *L'Etoile*, died during the voyage.

A FRIGATE

The *Boudeuse* was an armed frigate. These ships were fast, heavily armed naval vessels with many sails. They responded well to the person steering, but the high masts and complex rigging could cause problems. Reports at the time said that the *Boudeuse* sailed best of all with the wind from behind. She could reach a speed of 11 knots (12.7 miles per hour). French frigates were also lightly built. They were much lighter and less stiff than other ships of the time. This made them difficult to handle in heavy seas and more prone to wear and tear.

WEAPONS

The *Boudeuse* carried twenty-eight guns, each firing 12-pound shots. All were crammed onto one gun deck. The ship was not as long as many similar frigates and space was very limited.

CIRCUMNAVIGATION

Among the crew was a naturalist, who doubled as the ship's doctor, and an astronomer, who was also the pilot. The journey had scientific aims as well as political and military ones. The ship sailed to the Falkland Islands in the south Atlantic, around Cape Horn, and across the Pacific to Tahiti. De Bougainville was not the first European to reach the island, but he claimed Tahiti as French territory. A brother of a chief returned to France with him.

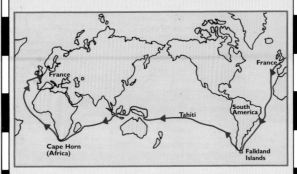

The route of the *Boudeuse*

LIFE ON BOARD

The ship was simply fitted out. All the men lived and slept on the deck below the gun deck. It had very little headroom — just five feet three inches from deck to ceiling. On this deck were live animals — cows, sheep, and pigs! The crowded conditions, poor hygiene, and bad, maggot-ridden food caused sickness. However, very few men died on the twenty-eight month voyage and most of these deaths were from accidents.

SHIPWORM

Instead of the copper sheave favored by other builders, a layer of tar protected the hull from attack in tropical waters.

DE BOUGAINVILLE

In 1782, de Bougainville commanded part of the fleet at the Battle of the Saints. In this Caribbean battle between the British and French fleets the French Admiral criticized him. He survived the criticism, and the French Revolution several years later, and rose to high office under Napoleon.

Batavia

Length
149 feet
182 feet with bowsprit

Width
34 feet 6 inches

Weight
640 tons

Mainmast
180 feet

Sails
Square rigged
10 in total

Crew
200 to 300 men

Weapons
32 cannons, of which 24 were cast iron. Variety of caliber, or barrel width, was typical of 17th-century weaponry.

Boudeuse

Length
130 feet

Width
33 feet

Weight
400 tons

Mainmast
131 feet

Sails
10 square-rigged, lateen, and
triangular foresails

Crew
230 men

Weapons
28 cannons

ENDEAVOUR

The *Endeavour* was the ship chosen by Captain James Cook in 1768 for the first of his three historic Pacific Ocean expeditions. Cook had been a merchant seaman who made coastal voyages carrying coal from the port of Whitby in Yorkshire. The *Endeavour* was a converted collier, a ship that transported coal. Colliers were small but very strong. The *Endeavour* was a wide ship, with a width almost one-third of her length. She had a shallow draft, so she could sail in coastal waters, but her extra width helped to make her stable in heavy seas.

FITTING OUT

The voyage of the *Endeavour* lasted nearly three years. It took two months to prepare the ship for sea. The builders protected her from attack by shipworm below the waterline. They nailed an extra layer of planks to the hull, over a coating of tar and horsehair. This extra wood skin was a cheaper solution than covering the hull with a layer of copper (see the lift-the-flap spread of the *Victory*). They built cabins for the officers and scientists on board and laid a new deck over the old coal hold. Cannons were dragged on board, and coal, wood, gunpowder, ropes, and sail canvas were stored in the holds. Barrels of preserved food, fresh water, beer, and wine (enough for ninety-four men for the voyage) were loaded aboard.

AIMS OF THE VOYAGE

The Royal Society in London persuaded the English Admiralty to support an expedition to Tahiti, in the Pacific Ocean, so that they could observe Venus passing between the Earth and the Sun. The Admiralty had its own reasons for the voyage. They wanted to restrict French influence (see *Boudeuse*), and Cook had secret orders to find the southern continent and claim it for England.

SCIENCE

This voyage was the first that had scientific discovery as the main objective. Trade and land seizure were less important. Sir Joseph Banks, a botanist, spent a huge sum — the equivalent of $800,000 in today's money — on equipment for the voyage. Banks named Botany Bay, in southeast Australia, after the wide variety of exotic plants found there.

The route of the *Endeavour*

CRAMPED SPACE

Imagining where everyone and everything fitted into the ship is difficult. The *Endeavour* had both a blacksmith's shop and a carpenter's shop. The scientists crammed in much medical, scientific, and botanical equipment alongside the stores. At one point in the voyage, the ship was home to seventeen sheep, several hens and ducks, a boar and sow, along with their litter of piglets, two dogs, and a goat!

HEALTH

Pickled cabbage, onions, and fresh fruit were among the supplies. Cook's insistence on a healthier diet, personal cleanliness, and fumigation of the ship kept the crew healthy, until they put into the port of Batavia (now Jakarta in Indonesia). Malaria and dysentery killed thirty-one crew members. In Cook's second great voyage, lasting three years, no one died of scurvy, thanks to a better diet and treatment with concentrated lemon juice.

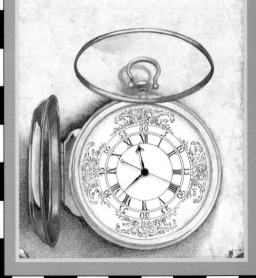

A chronometer. # This was a very accurate timepiece used for navigation.

VICTORY

The *Victory* is famous as the flagship of Admiral Horatio Nelson at the Battle of Trafalgar in 1805. She was launched in 1765. By the time of the battle, she was already forty years old, and had been refitted more than once.

A LARGE SHIP

In her day, the *Victory* was one of the largest ships afloat. She was built of wood. Twenty-five hundred oak trees were cut down to build this one ship.

ROPE

The shipbuilders needed a lot of rope, as well as timber, to build the ship. If all the rope used on board had been laid end to end, it would have stretched for twenty-eight miles. Rope had many different tasks on board. It controlled the sails that powered the ship and the direction in which the *Victory* sailed. Rope secured the ship's cannons and anchored the masts to the decks. The masts were very high and had to be firmly secured. Rope was also used to make climbing nets up the sides of the masts. The sailors used these nets to reach the tops of the masts.

NELSON

Horatio Nelson was the admiral in charge of the fleet at the Battle of Trafalgar. The *Victory* was his flagship, and the battle was his greatest victory. He defeated the joint fleets of the French and Spanish, but was fatally wounded in the battle.

TRAFALGAR

The two fleets fought the battle off the coast of southwest Spain, near Cape Trafalgar, on October 21, 1805. The English fleet sailed in two columns, side by side, at the center of the one line of enemy ships. They cut it in half and attacked both parts. More than 50 percent of the enemy ships were sunk or captured.

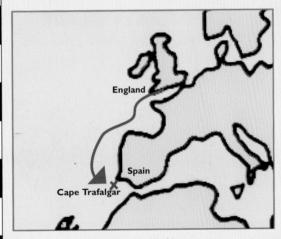

The *Victory*'s route to the Battle of Trafalgar

WEAPONS

The *Victory* was a warship. It had immense firepower. There were 106 cannons and 4 carronades on board. These ranged in size from small 2-inch barrels to massive 12-inch ones. They fired different weights of shots. The carronades were short-barreled iron guns, which fired monster 68-pound shots and caused great damage at close range.

Most of the cannons were placed on three gun decks below the main deck, and faced seaward through open gunports that could be closed to keep out seawater. Crew members mounted the cannons on sturdy wooden carriages with wheels. These would recoil, or jump violently backward, when fired. The gunpowder explosion in the barrel propelled them across the open gun decks, but thick rope tethers attached to the carriages stopped the cannons from crashing straight through the wooden sides of the ship.

The upper deck, or poop, of the *Victory* was armed with two 12-pounder cannons and two of the fearsome carronades. The uppermost deck, behind the mainmast, called the quarter deck, was armed with 12-pounder cannons. The fo'c'sle, or forecastle, just behind the foremast, had the same weapons as the poop.

The *Victory*, with three gun decks, was a ship of the line. These heavily armed ships formed a line in battle. They could use their guns to protect each other.

Endeavour

Length
97 feet

Width
29 feet

Weight
354 tons

Mainmast
85 feet

Sails
Square rigged, with two
triangular sails set on
the bowsprit, a pole facing
forward at the front of the ship

Crew
83 naval members, 11 scientists
and attendants

Weapons
10 cannons, 12 light rotating guns

GALVESTON

The *Galveston* was a typical fast-sailing slave ship from the last days of the slave trade. It was a clipper with several masts and many sails. The builders designed it for maximum speed, so that it could escape from government ships that were trying to stamp out the traffic in slaves.

THE SLAVE TRADE

The slave trade with America grew from the discoveries of European seamen. Since the early 1400s, the British, French, Dutch, Spanish, and Portuguese had all explored the coastline of West Africa. The aim of their voyages was to search for seagoing trade routes to East Asia. Nevertheless, their discoveries resulted in a tragic and brutal new trade in enslaved Africans.

Spain and Portugal were the first nations to seize slaves. In the early 1500s, the first ships, with their human cargo, crossed the Atlantic to Hispaniola. The other European sea powers soon followed, and demand for slaves grew rapidly in the new American colonies that needed a workforce. The first ship carrying slaves for the new colony of Virginia landed there in 1619.

TRIANGULAR TRADE

The slave trade was very efficient. Each stage of the voyage carried goods, or people, for sale. From Europe, the ships carried guns, gunpowder, cloth, knives, and liquor. Slave traders traded these goods in the African ports, then seized or purchased slaves and transported them across the Atlantic Ocean. This stage of the journey was called the "Middle Passage." It lasted from forty to sixty-nine days. Slave traders sold slaves on arrival, usually at an auction. In Caribbean ports, captains collected sugar, tobacco, molasses, cotton, and other agricultural products, and they shipped these back to Europe.

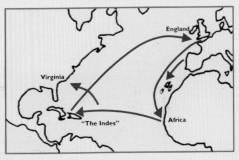

The slave trade

PROFIT

The British controlled the Caribbean islands and much of the American mainland until the Revolutionary War. British ports grew very rich on the slave trade. In 1800, more than 120 ships left Liverpool, England, alone and carried more than 30,000 slaves to the New World. The first slave ship out of Liverpool sailed in 1700. This one ship carried 220 slaves to Barbados, where the slaves were sold for a total of £4,239. We think that in the years of the slave trade more than 15 million black people were transported, with as many as 9 million dying on the voyages.

ON BOARD

Slave ships were brutal. Slaves were stripped naked, shackled, and packed into airless, cramped holds. Some ships included half decks, between the main decks, to fit more slaves into the ship. Slaves received two meals a day, usually consisting of rice, yams, and beans with some black bread and water.

ABOLITION

The trade lasted 350 years. It was abolished in 1815. Britain banned slavery in England and its colonies in 1833. During the American Civil War, President Abraham Lincoln issued the Emancipation Proclamation in 1863, which abolished slavery in the proslavery Confederate states. But American slavery did not actually end until 1865, when antislavery Union forces won the war.

Victory

Length
226 feet

Width
51 feet

Weight
2,425 tons

Mainmast
105 feet

Sails
10 square-rigged mainsails

Crew
850 to 900 men

Weapons
106 cannons, 4 carronades